Adventures in Heartlake City

Story and art by Blue Ocean

Friendship Fun written by Olivia London

Little, Brown Books for Young Readers
www.lbkids.co.uk

LITTLE, BROWN BOOKS FOR YOUNG READERS

First published in the US in 2015 by Little, Brown and Company
First published in the UK in 2015 by Hodder & Stoughton

1 3 5 7 9 10 8 6 4 2

LEGO, the LEGO logo, the FRIENDS logo and the Brick and Knob
configurations are trademarks of the LEGO Group.
Produced by Hodder & Stoughton under licence from the LEGO Group.
© 2015 The LEGO Group
Comic artwork © 2015 by Blue Ocean Entertainment AG, Germany

A CIP catalogue record for this book is available from the British Library.

ISBN 978-1-5102-0051-7

Printed and bound in the United States of America

Little, Brown Books for Young Readers
An imprint of Hachette Children's Group
Part of Hodder & Stoughton

Carmelite House
50 Victoria Embankment
London EC4Y 0DZ

An Hachette UK Company
www.hachette.co.uk

www.hachettechildrens.co.uk

Welcome to Heartlake City

Heartlake City is the home of LEGO Friends, five very different and very talented girls who are best friends. The city is centered around a heart-shaped lake (hence the name!), located directly between a beach and a mountain range. This location makes it perfect for all kinds of outdoor activities like flying, horse riding, dolphin observing, and more! The city itself is home to a mall, a café, a bakery, a vet, a beauty shop, a swimming pool, and adventure!

Great Places to Visit!

CLOVER MEADOWS
A place where people gather for picnics

CLEARSPRING MOUNTAINS
A mountain range with a spring

WHISPERING WOODS
A small forest in Heartlake City

MAIN STREET
A great place to hang out with your friends

HEARTLAKE STABLES
The horse stables that make up Summer Riding Camp

LAKE HEART
The heart-shaped lake in the center of the city, where people go to swim, fish, and ice skate

THE PARK
The Heartlake Do
Show is held here

HEARTLAKE HIGH
The local school attended by Andrea, Emma, Mia, Stephanie, and Olivia, and all of their friends

LIGHTHOUSE ISLAND
An island off the coast of Heartlake City

THE BEACH
The coastline. Emma and Olivia live near here.

Andrea

The musician of the group, Andrea is a talented singer and is great at making up her own songs. She loves anything that pertains to music: singing, playing the piano, dancing, and the theater. But she is a great cook and works at a café. She also has a not-so-secret love of bunnies.

Emma

Emma is a very trendy girl who loves style. Definitely the fashionista of the group, she enjoys fashion design, making jewelry, interior design, and makeovers. She's also a fan of English horseback jumping and karate. She is sometimes forgetful and unable to speak up for herself, but she's a wonderful friend.

Mia

The animal lover of the group, Mia is a vegetarian. She enjoys taking care of and spending time with lots and lots of animals. She also excels at sports, drumming, and training animals. She spends her free time horse riding, camping, and doing magic tricks.

Olivia

Olivia loves science, nature, and history. If she could, she would spend all day inventing new things, as well as taking pictures and drawing. Super intelligent and focused, Olivia is quite a brain. She's still clumsy sometimes, but who isn't?

Stephanie

A confident natural leader, Stephanie is very social, creative, and organized. She loves planning events, parties, and soccer. She enjoys talking to people, writing stories, and dancing ballet. She is very down-to-earth, though at times a little bossy.

Friendship Tree in Danger

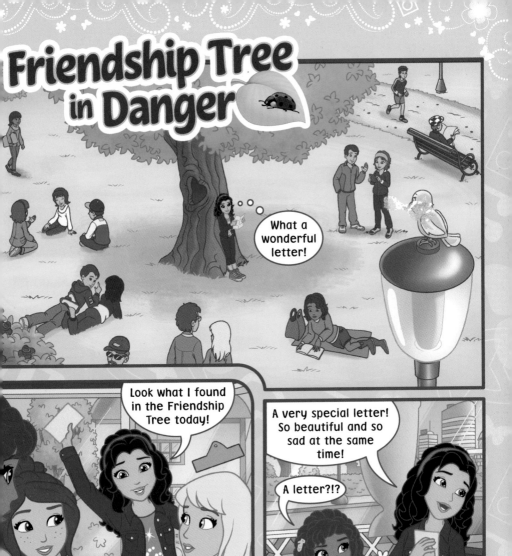

What a wonderful letter!

Look what I found in the Friendship Tree today!

A very special letter! So beautiful and so sad at the same time!

A letter?!?

Tom's father is a writer. They are both traveling around the world in search of special stories.

But Tom is terribly lonely because they never stay anywhere for very long and he has no friends.

...many birds and squirrels live in the park!

And the tree has created so many friendships for people!

I know. But Heartlake City needs the new highway.

Can't it be built somewhere else?

That would be much too expensive. I'm really very sorry!

What are we going to do now?

We mustn't give up.

We'll follow the Friendship Tree's example: We'll connect the whole city!

I've got it!!!

5 Awesome Ways to Help!

How Can YOU Make a Difference?

When Emma and her friends found out that the Friendship Tree was in danger of being cut down, they sprang into action to help save the tree. Have you ever wanted to do something to make a difference in your community but you didn't know how to get started? Now you do! Whether you want to start a recycling program, help raise money for charity, or donate things to people in need—no matter what the cause—there's always something you can do to help.

Check out this list of **5 Awesome Ways to Help** and get started making a change in your hometown!

1: Learn All About It

It's super important to educate yourself on whatever cause you're trying to help. The more you know, the more you can teach other people about why caring for this cause is so important. You can do research on the computer, ask your teacher to recommend some books on the subject, or go to the library and search for them yourself.

2: Spread the Word

Now that you know a lot about the cause you are trying to help, spread the word to other people and explain why this cause needs their help, too. You can do this by simply starting a conversation with a friend about the subject, talking to your teacher about including it in one of your school lessons, or even filming a video of yourself talking about the cause and showing it to friends and family.

3: Volunteer

There are already many ways to volunteer in your community, so ask your parents or a teacher to help you find the type of volunteer activity that is right for you. Giving your time is so rewarding, and every little bit counts.

4: Throw a Fundraiser * * ❤ 🦋

Just like the LEGO Friends who helped save their tree, you can have your own fundraiser to help raise money for your cause. It can be as small as having a bake sale or a lemonade stand on your front lawn and donating the money you make, or talking to your teacher or principal about organizing something larger in your school. Some great ideas for fundraisers include talent shows, carnivals, fashion shows, or sports events. You can sell tickets and food, and raffle off prizes—all for a cause!

5: Write a Letter 🦋 ❤ *

Writing a letter to a local government official, newspaper editor, or city council member is an important way to make a difference. You're not the only one who thinks your cause is important. If everyone who thinks your cause is important writes a letter, that's a lot of letters! Together, they can all make a difference.

Lion in Distress

THE FRIENDS ARE WORKING AT THE JUNGLE RESCUE BASE THIS SUMMER, BUT MIA WORKS THE HARDEST AND LONGEST.

We've hardly seen each other in the last few days! You're working 24/7!

I know, but it's just such great fun!

Yesterday, I joined the patrol and we watched wild tigers.

Cool! I'd like to see them, too!

Well, then let's make a patrol together! Maybe we'll discover something exciting!

Yeah, that's a great idea!

TODAY, MIA HAS A PARTICULARLY NICE JOB.

You'll soon be well again and then you can go back to your mommy.

SLURP
SLURP

More About Lions

The King of the Jungle

The lion is known as the king of the jungle for its courage and beauty, even though it doesn't actually live in the jungle. Lions live in southern Africa—in the Sahara—in eastern Africa, and some parts of India. Did you know that lions are the only kind of cats that live in groups? A group of lions is called a "pride." A pride is made up of a family of lions. These prides, which can be as large as fifteen or twenty lions, are made up mostly of female lions and their young, and usually have between one and three male lions leading the

Peter Schwarz/Shutterstock.com

group. Female lions are the pride's hunters (cool, huh?), while the male lions protect and defend the pride from attackers. When a female lion gives birth to her cubs, she hides them from the pride for up to six weeks to protect them from the other members of the pride. You're probably wondering why she does this, aren't you? She hides her cubs because grown lions will harm cubs that they don't recognize immediately as family. The mother will only visit her cubs to feed them. It's lucky that cubs are born with spotted coats so they can blend in with their habitats! (Actually, it's not *exactly* luck; it's the way nature works.) When the mother is ready to introduce them to the pride, she must do so carefully—very carefully!

Stuart G Porter/Shutterstock.com

Fab Facts:

- ✿ A lion's roar can be heard from five miles away!
- ✿ Male lions can be up to eight feet long and can weigh up to five hundred pounds.
- ✿ Lion cubs are born blind.
- ✿ The lion's mane only grows on male lions and can be used to scare away attackers or to attract female lions.

Yes, a cat, cute. *Sigh!*

Puddycat! Puddycat!

Puddycat! Come here!

Anna, honey, come now. The others are already at the playground!

Nice puddycat!

Oh, you two look so sweet!

stroke

FORTUNATELY, ANNA FINALLY ALLOWS OLIVIA TO HEAD FOR THE PLAYGROUND.

...op, little ...nny, hop hop!

There you are at last!

Tee-hee

Hop Hop

Better late than never. Everything okay with you?

Great! The boys are digging in the sand and Josie is swinging.

Higher! Higher! Up to the clouds!

Eh, do you think that sand is unhealthy?

What?!? Why?

Oooooooh!

Munch munch

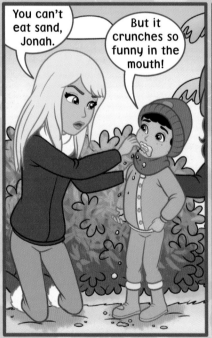

You can't eat sand, Jonah.

But it crunches so funny in the mouth!

Josie, what happened to Anna?!

I did her hair! It's so pretty now!

I'm a princess!

I'm thirsty!

Stephanie, I need the toilet!

I wanna stay at the playground!

Oh dear! What are we going to do now?

LUCKILY, THERE'S A SUPERMARKET NEARBY.

Stephanie, why don't you take Josie to the supermarket while I wait here with the others?

Okay!

Come on, Josie. You can go to the bathroom there and I'll buy something to drink.

THE VISIT TO THE SUPERMARKET WAS WORTHWHILE.

I wanna do a picnic!

What a great idea, Josie! Let's do this!

We've brought things for a picnic and...

...Olivia, is something wrong?

Forget the picnic! Anna has disappeared!!!

Calm down. When did you last see Anna?

Just a few seconds ago in the sandbox!

I was taking a photo of the children and suddenly she disappeared!!!

Then she can't have gone very far.

Let me see the pictures you took!

Here! Although I really can't see how that could help!

Well, I do!

Look who's also in the picture!

I don't believe it: the cat!!!

OLIVIA HEARS A HAPPY CHUCKLE FROM BEHIND THE BUSHES.

Anna, here you are!

I'm here. Puddycat is here, too.

Meow!

Look who I found! I was so worried!

There you are! Here, Anna, take a pretzel!

Yay, pretzel!

Mmmm, yummy!

Tee-hee. Tastes better than sand. Right, Jonah?

I'll say one thing: In the future we're only looking after two children. At the very most!

Agreed. I'm worn out! Babysitting certainly isn't child's play!

End

Want a Job?

Start Your Own Business!

If you love kids as much as Olivia and Stephanie do, babysitting will be a great job for you—one day! Watching kids is a *huge* responsibility and a lot of work. For now, you'd probably have more fun building your skills by creating a small business. Just follow these steps to help you launch your first career today! (Make sure you talk to your parents first. Involving your guardians guarantees a safe and fun business!)

What's the Job?!

First, you should consider your interests. If you like pets, you could start walking dogs or feeding the neighbors' cats when they are out of town. If you like cooking, you could sell cookies or open a lemonade stand. If you like computers, you could teach your grandparents how to use e-mail. If you can't think of a business, maybe discuss it with your parents. You and one of your guardians or siblings could create a business together.

You Name It!

The name of your business is something you're going to use a lot, so it should be a name that you like! Pick something that's easy to understand and remember but also has a little flair. Try to choose something catchy. Write down some options and then ask your friends to vote on their faves! Here're a few that might be fun to try:

- ✿ Dana's Dog-Walking Service
- ✿ Snack Time Stand—Lemonade and Cookies by Amy
- ✿ E-mail 101
- ✿ Melanie the Chore Helper!

Got a Logo?

Most businesses have a logo or icon, which is an image people recognize as belonging to that business or product, like the recognizable red icon that represents LEGO. What do you want your logo to look like?

What's Your Business Motto? 🦋

It's your business, so what are the top five things you would want people who hire you to know about your service and what you offer? In other words, why should they hire YOU? Write down five things and make sure you tell people when they ask about your business. Check out the sample motto below:

> ✿ "I am responsible, clean, helpful, organized, and thoughtful!"

Spread the Word! ♥ 🦋

When you start a new business, you need to market it. When you "market" something, you are spreading the word about it so people know you're there. Jot down some ways you would market your new business! Who would you tell and how?

Hint #1: Think about the types of people who will be hiring you, and then figure out how you can best reach those people.

Hint #2: Don't market to strangers. It's better to stay close to home, and always make sure your guardians know where they can find you.

Here are some suggestions of people to market your business to:

- ✿ Family and extended family
- ✿ Friends and friends' families
- ✿ Friends of your parents
- ✿ Neighbors
- ✿ Teachers

Design a Poster!

In order to spread the word about a business, many people design posters. When placed in your neighborhood or a community center, they can be seen by a lot of people. Remember not to give out your personal contact information. It is better for strangers to go through your parents or guardian. (Remember, it's always a good idea to involve an adult to keep yourself safe!)

You can also make a digital "flyer" and send it to your friends and family in an e-mail blast.

What would your first poster look like? Some information to include:

- ✿ The name of your service
- ✿ How to contact you
- ✿ What you charge for your service
- ✿ When your service is available

Enchanting Penguins

THIS WEEK AT SCHOOL, STUDENTS GET TO TRY OUT THEIR DREAM JOBS. MIA HAS BEEN WAITING ANXIOUSLY FOR DAYS TO FIND OUT IF SHE GOT THE ONE SHE WANTED...

Hurray!!! I got the internship at the zoo!

And I'm going to a computer firm that develops apps!

I'm working with the editorial team of my favorite st magazine. How cool is that?!?

I get to look over the shoulder of a designer at work.

I'm working at the cake shop!

I'm so stoked about this! I've always dreamed of being a vet and now I can watch the zoo veterinarian for a whole week.

It's definitely going to be a very special week for all of us.

THE NEXT MORNING, MIA IS WELCOMED BY SIMON, THE ZOOKEEPER.

Oh, wow. I've never seen real elephants so close before! Can I touch them?

You have to! You'll help me patch them up.

My goodness, he's huge! What's wrong with him?

He is a *she*! Mimi has an inflamed toenail.

She's really gentle. You can come in, Mia.

Seriously?

See!

Pat Pat

Hi, Mimi. Nice to meet you.

I never imagined such large creatures could be so gentle. This is a dream come true.

41

That's terrible! This is their home. The baby penguins were born here. They shouldn't have to leave their home just because of money.

I know, but the zoo only has so much funding. If only the pengu habitat drew more visitors

Somehow they look sad. As if they knew...

Waddle Waddle

MIA HAS A GIRLS' NIGHT WITH STEPHANIE THE NEXT EVENING.

Today I learned a hundred new recipes. My cupcakes will be unbeatable! Mia, you seem distracted.

Oh... It was so nice at the zoo. Until Simon told me that the penguins have to go.

THE FATE OF THE PENGUINS IS ON MIA'S MIND ALL OF THE NEXT DAY.

I have to help the penguins But how???

SUDDENLY, ON HER LUNCH BREAK...

That's it!!!

Maxim Ma
The greatest m

THE NEXT DAY...

...Ta-da! One of the rings is no longer attached to the others!

Click

Bravo!

CLAP CLAP

CLAP CLAP

WOW!

Oh hey, you littl party crasher! Wh are you doing here?

Waddle Waddle

CLAP CLAP

Look! Her magic assistant is a penguin!!

AFTER THE SHOW...

He follows me at every turn.

You'd best take him home with you. Tee-hee!

That won't b necessa

Meet Jane Goodall

Animal Researcher

Mia isn't the first girl to dream of working with animals. One young girl who dreamed of working with chimpanzees from a very young age not only grew up to live out her dream but also became one of the world's most famous animal researchers!

Jane Goodall was born on April 3, 1934, in London, England. When she was only one year old, Jane received a stuffed animal chimpanzee from her father that she named Jubilee and carried with her everywhere. At a young age, she realized her love for animals and her desire to work with chimpanzees in particular. At the age of twenty-three, Jane moved to Africa to study chimpanzees in the wild!

LeonP/Shutterstock.com

This was a long time ago, so not much was known about how chimpanzees behaved or interacted with one another in their own habitats. When Jane went to live on the farm of a friend in the Kenya highlands, it soon led her to venture into the forests of Tanzania to study the chimpanzees firsthand. Scientists thought that humans were the only species to make tools for certain things like eating, building, or gathering food. Jane discovered on one of her visits to the forest that the chimpanzees were doing just that—they made tools out of tree branches for fishing insects out of holes!

Attila Kisbenedek/AFP/Getty Images

Another important discovery made by Jane was that chimpanzees weren't actually vegetarians like most scientists thought. Instead, they ate small animals. She also observed that they had a basic language that they used to communicate, which was made up of about twenty different sounds. Jane worked with chimpanzees her whole life, and in her later years became known throughout the world for her expertise.

If you love animals as much as Jane did, go learn more about all the different kinds of animal professions you can have one day!

Trip to Winter Wonderland

THE FRIENDS ARE SPENDING THE WEEKEND IN THE MOUNTAINS SO OLIVIA CAN TEACH THE GIRLS HOW TO SNOWBOARD.

OLIVIA SLEPT BADLY LAST NIGHT.

The others aren't having any fun. This isn't what I had in mind...

That's it! After all, we've come here to have some fun *together*!

Woof!

Woof!

Girls, forget snowboarding!

What would you girls like to do?

Build snowmen!

Play in the snow!

Snowball fight!

Let's go sledding!

Attack!!!

Just you wait!

SPLAT!

Tee-hee!

AND SO THE FRIENDS HAVE A PERFECT WEEKEND IN THE SNOW AFTER ALL...

End

Fun with Friends!

Snowed In?!

The LEGO Friends had great weather for snowboarding, but have you ever been snowed (or rained) in? It can feel like you have nothing fun to do. But here are a few entertaining ways to pass the time indoors with your best friends!

It's a Sing-Off! ✽ 🦋 ✽

Sit in a circle and go around it clockwise or counter-clockwise. The first person starts singing a song, and the person next to her needs to listen for a word or phrase in the song's lyrics that she knows exists in the lyrics of a different song. Once she hears that word or phrase, she jumps in and begins to sing a new song. If she can't think of something before the first person finishes her song, she's out! Keep going around the circle until there's a winner!

Screen Test

Write the names of your
favorite movies or TV shows on
pieces of paper, fold them in
half, and then put them in a hat
and mix them up. The first person
will pick a piece of paper randomly
and then has to act out a scene from
the movie or show for her friends! Whoever guesses
the correct answer goes next. Then she picks a new
movie or show from the hat and acts out a new scene.
You can also change the category to favorite songs,
animals, or celebrities!

Build It!

Grab your LEGO bricks and challenge
one another to some building games!
Use a stopwatch to time one another
and see who can build the fastest
LEGO Friends set from the instructions.
Or everyone study a small LEGO build for
thirty seconds, and then hide it. Now try
to build it from memory. A third fun
game using your LEGO sets would
be to give everyone a blindfold and
have them build something without
using their eyes! It's not easy!

Girl Talk

Sure, you talk to your friends all the time, but have you ever wanted to share something really special with them and not found the right moment? Here's your chance! Go around in a circle and share a secret that you've never shared before and see how much closer together it brings you.

Write a Story! *

Grab a notepad. Someone will start by writing the first sentence of a story. They pass the notepad, and the next person writes the next sentence. Go around and around until you and your friends have created a story. Now, read it aloud.

It's All About Fun!

Friends are for-e-e-e-ver!

Tomorrow we can rehearse the whole thing on the stage. See ya!

THE NEXT DAY, THE GIRLS REHEARSE ON THE SCHOOL STAGE.

Let's have a look at the stage!

Look, Emma! Our own dressing table!

We're like real stars!

Boy oh boy! That's a lot of chairs!!!

Don't just stand around—unpack your instruments!

Everyone ready?

Click

Just a moment, nearly done.

One, two, three, four!

Everywhere we goooo... *croak!!!*

What was that? Did you swallow a crow?

Cough!...I'm fine now.

THE NEXT ATTEMPT...

S-Sor
I'm a
nervo

Emma! Are you playing for the first time?

Why? Nobody's here!

But the whole school will be watching us.

It was much cozier in our garage.

Yeah, I felt more confident there.

Okaaay, let's finish fo today and tr again tomorro

What's YOUR Band?

A Fun Quiz!

Ever wanted to be a star? Here's your chance to find out what music fits your personality! Just answer these questions and start rockin'!

1. What kind of music do you like to listen to?
   - A. Really loud with LOTS of guitar—who needs to hear the words?
   - B. Pretty lyrics, soft melody
   - C. Something I can dance to!

2. How would you name your band?
   - A. Take two crazy words and put them together
   - B. Choose something that inspires me
   - C. After me, obviously!

3. What would one of your concerts be like?

    A. There would be a lot of screaming fans bumping into one another.

    B. It would be in a small café with just me and my fans.

    C. It would be a huge performance with dance routines and costumes!

4. What instrument do you play?

    A. Electric guitar or drums

    B. Acoustic guitar and vocals

    C. Just my voice!

ANSWERS:

A's: If you chose mostly A's, you're in a serious rock or metal band. You like loud music, screaming lyrics, and hyper fans!

B's: If you chose mostly B's, you're in a folk rock band. You like smaller shows, soulful lyrics, and fans who like to listen.

C's: If you chose mostly C's, you're a pop star all the way! You love putting on a show and being at the center of it.

A Difficult Decision

What's that, Mia?

A letter from a company that does hot-air-balloon trips.

HURRAY! I've won!!! I'm going for a ride in a hot-air balloon!!!

Ohhh, that's great!

My dream has come true: next week I'll be flying like a bird above Heartlake City!

Cool! That sounds like so much fun!

I wish I'd won.

I've always wanted to do this!

Yes, it must be fantastic to sail weightlessly through the sky!

What I would give to experience that...

Oh no! All my friends want to go, but I can only take two people with me.

NEXT DAY AT SCHOOL...

I love all my friends so much. How can I pick just two?

Hey, Mia! You know that book you've been wanting to read? I bought you a copy.

Oh— thanks!

Mia! Want to go horseback riding today?

Yes, sur I'd love

AT HOME...

My new cupcake recipe is great! Do you wanna come over and try some?

I'm sorry, Stephanie, but I'm going riding today.

Hey, Mia. What about a movie this evening?

Great idea. I'm dying to watch that new comedy!

Decisions, Decisions

A Bit of Advice

Have you ever had to make a hard decision like Mia did in this story? Who should you invite to your birthday party? Should you use your allowance to buy an expensive item, or should you save your money? Would it be more fun to spend the weekend at the beach or at an amusement park?

Decisions can be tricky, and sometimes it's hard to know if you're making the right one. It's especially hard when your friends are involved and you don't want to hurt someone's feelings. Here are some things you can do to help yourself in difficult situations.

Ask Someone You Trust

If you're having trouble making a decision, get another perspective. Asking for help is always a good plan when you have to make an important decision. Parents and grandparents are usually the best people to ask. They have a lot of "life experience," and they'll have your best interests in mind when they consider your decision.

This person could also be an older sibling, a good friend, or even a teacher. Any of these people probably won't tell you exactly what to do, but they'll help guide you toward the best decision for *you*—because they know you so well!

Make a List of Pros and Cons

Divide a piece of paper into two even sections. On one side, write down all the positive things about your decision. On the other side, write down all the negative things about making that same decision. Then compare your lists to see which is longer. If something has more negatives than positives, avoid it! You can do this for all the options you have until you find the best answer to your problem.

Research

Another great method for making a decision is investigating your options. For instance, if you can't decide between going to the beach or going to an amusement park, learn more about both places. You should consider things like cost, travel, and of course, what sounds more fun to you. After educating yourself about your decision, it usually becomes much easier to decide.

BUT THE NEXT DAY, SHE FORGETS AND GOES TO THE STABLE.

Today is going to be a good practice. I can feel it.

Mia! I thought we had plans to go riding together today?

Oh no! I totally forgot about that!!!

Can we postpone it? I've only just started jumping.

Oh, all right, then. But please don't stand me up next time!

ON THE NEXT DAY!

Hurray! A clear round, Bella!!!

Whinny!

You can tell that we train every day. We're getting better and better!

Mia, where were you yesterday?!? We waited in the garden for you!

Garden?!? Oh no, I totally forgot about it!!! I'm sorry!

All you think about is riding...

Riding? Oh no! The tournament! I'm late. Let's talk about it tomorrow!

Mia has nothing but riding on her mind. It's really annoying!

It's like her friends don't even matter.

Stomp Stomp

Come on, don't be like that! Mia just wants to do well at the tournament.

Right! If the tournament is so important to Mia, we should support her.

Exactly. We can't give up on our friends so easily.

Friends Forever

More Advice

Friends are some of the most important people in our lives. They know our deepest secrets, share in our celebrations, and are there for us when we're sad. But did you know that keeping a friendship in good shape takes some work? Every friendship needs to be given attention, care, and love for it to grow strong and last forever. If you and one of your friends get into a fight, or you just want to strengthen the bonds you already have, these creative activities are great ways to strengthen your friendship bond!

Write a Note

Write your friend a note telling her something about her that you love. It could be about how funny she is, or how she always lets you borrow her clothes, or even how much she knows about math! Have her do the same for you and then exchange them!

Share a Good and Bad Moment

Share a time when your friend helped you with a problem or made you feel better about something when you were sad. Tell her how much this meant to you. Then share a time when you might have been hurt by something she did and explain to her why. Have her do the same. This exercise will help you appreciate the good times and help you learn from your mistakes so you become the best friends you can be!

Just the Two of You

Take some time to plan a special activity to share together. This could be making each other matching friendship bracelets, going to a movie or concert together, or having a friendship slumber party! Just choose something to celebrate how wonderful your friendship is and how happy you are to have found each other.

Make a Friendship Album *

Put together a photo album of your friendship. Use as many pictures as you can find from the time your friendship began until now, and write down where you were, what you were doing, and when each picture was taken. Be sure to include silly stories, too. You can make one album to share, or you can make two different ones so you can each have one to keep!